Ghost Wolf

Ghost Wolf

Karleen Bradford

Illustrations by Allan Cormack
and Deborah Drew-Brook

ORCA BOOK PUBLISHERS

Library and Archives Canada Cataloguing in Publication
Bradford, Karleen

Ghost wolf / Karleen Bradford;
illustrations by Allan Cormack and Deborah Drew-Brook.
(Orca echoes)

ISBN 10: 1-55143-341-9 / ISBN 13: 978-155143-341-7

I.Cormack, Allan
II. Drew-Brook, Deborah   III. Title.   IV. Series.

PS8553.R217G48 2005   jC813'.54   C2005-904069-6

First Published in the United States: 2005
Library of Congress Control Number: 2005929688

Summary: Matt is starting to fit in at camp when he makes a blunder that sends him
on a midnight quest from which only a ghost wolf can lead him to safety.

Orca Book Publishers gratefully acknowledges the support for its publishing programs
provided by the following agencies: the Government of Canada through the Book Publishing
Industry Development Program and the Canada Council for the Arts, and the Province of
British Columbia through the BC Arts Council and the Book Publishing Tax Credit.

Design and layout by Lynn O'Rourke

Cover and interior illustrations by Allan Cormack and Deborah Drew-Brook

Orca Book Publishers   Orca Book Publishers
PO Box 5626, Stn. B   PO Box 468 ·
Victoria, BC Canada   Custer, WA USA
V8R 6S4   98240-0468

www.orcabook.com
Printed and bound in Canada.
Printed on 100% PCW recycled paper.
11 10 09 08 • 5 4 3 2

For Eric, Ava, Thea and Gavin

Chapter One
Camp

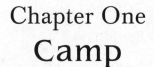

"It will be great, Matt!"

His dad's words rang in his ears. Matt stood in his cabin doorway and watched the car drive away.

"I loved this camp when I was a kid," his father had told him. "You will too. Just wait and see."

Matt kept his back turned to the other kids. He was not going to let them see him cry! But after the car drove out of sight, he felt a big, painful lump right where his heart should be. He'd never been good at outdoors stuff. He wasn't sure about this at all.

In the cabin it sounded like a whole army of boys were fighting over the bunks they wanted. A counselor's voice rang out.

"Okay, guys, enough! Tim, you're a big guy. You take a bottom bunk. Don't want you crashing down on the kid beneath you. Rupal, you take the top one. Joey, the other top one."

The three boys settled down and began to make up their bunks.

"And you...Matt!"

Matt wiped at his eyes and turned around.

"Matt, you get the bottom one over there under Joey."

There were six boys in the cabin. The two others had taken the last bunks. One boy was already on the top one, the other on the bottom. Matt was surprised to see that they were twins.

"Sandy, Tommy, I can't tell you two apart," the counselor said. "Looks like you're all set up. Great!"

Matt dumped his bedroll on his bunk. He was glad he had been given a corner one. He crawled in to spread out his sleeping bag, and it was like a cozy, dark cave.

He didn't have much chance to enjoy it, though.

"Listen up," the counselor said. "My name is Dave. I'm in charge of this cabin. That's my bunk over by the window. First off, you all have to know the rules. Then you have to obey them. Anyone who doesn't gets sent home."

Getting sent home sounded pretty good to Matt, but he listened. Camp was going to be hard enough. He didn't want to get in trouble too. His dad would hate it if he were sent home. The problem was, Matt always forgot things.

Matt was too nervous to eat much dinner that night. The singsong around the campfire was fun, but when they went back to the cabin he got nervous again. He crawled into his sleeping bag. The counselor, Dave, stood by the door.

"Lights out now," Dave said. He waited for a minute and went out.

Soon Matt heard a quiet whisper.

"That guy's going to be a pain!" It was the boy named Tim. "Rules, rules, rules. Who cares about stupid rules anyway? Not me, that's for sure. I do what I want."

Joey whispered from the top bunk. "Yeah, right," he said. He didn't sound like he believed Tim.

Matt listened as the others squirmed into their sleeping bags. He had never shared a room before. It felt strange. He thought about his room at home. He thought about all his airplanes and spacecraft models. He thought about the star charts on his walls. He missed it.

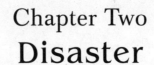

Chapter Two
Disaster

A shrill whistle woke Matt the next morning. It startled him so much that he leapt out of bed. Thank goodness he was in the bottom bunk! But being in the bottom bunk was the last good thing that happened to him that day.

"Up and at 'em," Dave ordered. "Wash up and get ready for breakfast." His voice was cheery and friendly, but it didn't make Matt feel better at all.

After breakfast they lined up to get their life jackets. They were going to learn to canoe.

"Wow," crowed Tim. "I've always wanted to paddle a canoe! How cool is that?"

Dave took them out one at a time. By the end of the morning, all the boys were allowed to go out by themselves. They just had to stay inside the markers. All the boys, that is, but Matt.

"You'd better stick with me for a while," Dave said. Matt had tipped the canoe twice and crashed it into the dock. The water was only waist deep, but they had both got soaked. Tim paddled over to them when they were righting the canoe. He circled around them with no problem at all.

"What's the matter, dummy?" he said, laughing at Matt.

"That's enough, Tim," Dave said.

Matt was sure he saw Tim stick his tongue out at Dave as he paddled away.

"Hey, Matt," Dave said to him, "don't worry about it. I'll bet you're a great swimmer."

Matt's heart sank. He'd had swimming lessons at home. He couldn't even float. No matter how hard he tried, he ended up with a mouthful of water.

Sure enough, he had to touch his feet to the bottom twice before he could make it out to the dock. The twins already had their junior swimming badges. They were as happy in the water as seals.

"Come on, Matt," they said. "It's easy. Just relax."

But it wasn't easy for Matt. It wasn't easy at all.

Tim teased him all afternoon. The teasing only made Matt more clumsy. He tripped on his way to the table at dinner. His food flew all over the place.

"That's okay, Matt," Dave said. "Sometimes it takes a while to get used to things." The words were kind, but even Dave seemed to be losing patience.

"What a loser," Tim said as soon as Dave was out of hearing.

Matt flushed bright red.

That night, Matt curled up tight in his sleeping bag. He felt about as rotten as he ever had in his life. Then he heard a whisper.

"Matt?"

He sat up.

"I've got something for you," Joey hissed from the top bunk.

An object landed on Matt's bed with a thunk. Matt smelled the good, rich smell of chocolate. A chocolate bar! The big lump in his chest shrank a little bit. Maybe things would get better.

"Thanks," he hissed back. He tucked the chocolate bar under his pillow. He would eat it later. For now, he would just smell it for a while.

The others fell asleep right away, but Matt lay awake in the dark.

Thank goodness the camp was only for two weeks. If only they didn't have to go on a two-day tenting trip at the end. They were going to paddle across lakes. They were going to portage the canoes between the campsites. He was just a kid. How was he supposed to carry a canoe?

Then he sat up straight in his bunk again. Was that a howl in the distance? He stuck his head out into the room and listened. It came again. Was it a wolf?

It sounded as lonely as he was.

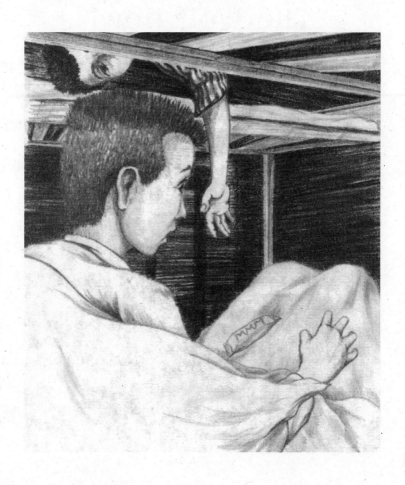

Chapter Three
The Wolf Howl

Two weeks later, Matt wasn't lonely anymore.

He had made friends with Joey. He had forgotten his paddle at the start of the camping trip, but the twins had brought it to him before anyone else noticed. They had become good friends too. And Rupal knew so many jokes! Matt laughed at his jokes so much that he forgot to worry. Camp was way more fun than he had thought it would be.

Except for Tim. Tim never stopped teasing him. Matt was learning how to do things pretty well. But whenever Tim started teasing him, he forgot and made mistakes.

To his surprise, he liked camping. He was good at setting up the tent he shared with Joey and Rupal. He was strong too. He could even help Dave carry their canoe. Sometimes he felt proud of himself.

It was the last night of the camping trip. Matt sat between Rupal and Joey around the fire. They were toasting marshmallows. He felt warm and happy. The flames from the campfire sparked up into the dark sky. Matt hunched over and waved his marshmallow stick around a bit. The gooey, half-burned blob slipped off the end and fell into the fire with a sizzle. Matt sighed, but he didn't really care. He leaned back and looked up at the night sky. He could see everything so clearly here. He knew the names of the stars and the planets by heart, but in the city he could never see them.

"One last song," Dave announced. He began to belt out the words. Matt joined in. He liked singing too. When the last notes died away, everyone fell silent. Matt was getting sleepy.

Then his eyes shot open. From close by, a long, singing howl went up. He hadn't heard that sound since the first night.

"That's a wolf!" Dave exclaimed.

A couple of the boys jumped to their feet. Dave stopped them.

"Wait, guys. Just listen!"

"But what if it comes to get us?" A frightened whisper.

Matt smiled in the darkness. That was Tim's voice. He didn't sound so brave now.

"Don't worry," Dave answered. "It's just calling to its friends. Listen," he repeated.

The boys fell silent.

The wolf howled again.

"My dad saved a wolf once," Matt said. He was surprised to hear himself speak. He hadn't meant to.

"How did he do that?" Dave asked.

Matt didn't answer. The guys would just laugh at him. But Dave urged him on.

"How did your dad save a wolf?" he asked again.

"Come on, Matt, tell us," Sandy and Tommy said together.

"Okay," Matt said. "It was like this," he began.

Chapter Four
His Dad's Story

"My dad used to come to this camp when he was a kid," Matt said. "Then he came as a counselor. He even came as a director the year before he married my mom. That's why he sent me here. He wanted me to get to know the place because he liked it so much." Matt stopped. His cheeks flamed. He was glad no one could see him blushing in the dark.

"Go on," Joey said. "What happened?" He gave Matt a friendly poke.

Matt drew a deep breath.

"One time, my dad heard something when he was following a trail through the woods," he said.

"Something like a whine. He followed the noise. After a while, he found a wolf caught in a leghold trap. It was a big wolf, all white. My dad said it was a young one."

Matt found the words more easily now. In his mind he could hear his dad telling the story. "The wolf was in really bad shape. My dad felt sorry for it. He wanted to help. He got closer and closer. He thought the wolf would jump at him, but the wolf just lay there. He looked at my dad with big, yellow eyes. My dad said there was something about those eyes. The wolf just stared and stared at him. Like he was trying to talk to him. And the wolf didn't act scared at all. My dad got so close that he could touch the trap. The wolf still didn't move."

The other boys looked at Matt. Their eyes were wide in the firelight. No one said a word. Matt went on.

"My dad knows about traps, and he doesn't like them. He released the catch and set the wolf free.

For a moment the wolf just lay there. My dad was afraid the wolf was going to go for him. But the wolf just got to his feet, looked at my dad again and melted into the woods."

"I don't believe it," Tim said. "That never happened."

"It did!" Matt said.

"If Matt says it happened, then it did," Joey said.

"Right," said Rupal.

Chapter Five
Out After Dark

"Why didn't the wolf attack him?" Tim demanded. "And why would anyone want to save a wolf anyway?"

"Hey, Tim," Dave said, "wolves have gotten a bad rap. They're not all killers, you know. In fact, hardly any wolves are left in some places now. Lots of people want to save them. Just listen," he added. "Listen to how cool it sounds."

The wolf howled and howled. To Matt it sounded lonely and sad. At last the howls died away.

"That was really strange," Dave said. "I've never heard a wolf howling like that. And there was only one. Usually there are more." He listened again.

When he was sure the wolf had stopped calling, he turned to the boys. "Time for bed, guys. We have an early start tomorrow."

They covered the remains of the fire with sand and headed for their tents.

"That was a good story, Matt," Joey said sleepily. "Good night."

"Yeah," Rupal said. "Good night."

"Good night," Matt said.

Soon everyone else was asleep. But now Matt wasn't sleepy at all. He lay awake, listening for the wolf, but it didn't howl again. He turned over and snuggled down into his sleeping bag. He heard the wind blowing. He saw the moon through the small window in the tent. He smelled the pine trees. It was nice. He rolled over again. He had to get to sleep. They had a long paddle back to the camp the next day. He didn't want to be tired.

Matt's heart leapt. He sat bolt upright. His life jacket! He had left it at the beginning of the portage from the last lake! He had been thinking about going home. He and Joey had been making plans about when they could see each other again. He had completely forgotten about his life jacket.

Why was he always forgetting things?

His heart sank down into his stomach like a piece of lead. None of the mistakes he had made yet had been half this bad. He couldn't do anything right! Now he had spoiled everything. He would have to go all the way back for the life jacket in the morning. They would all have to wait for him.

Then he had an idea. He looked around in the dark. The others were breathing deeply—they were all sound asleep. As quietly as he could, he reached his arm into his pack. His hand closed around his flashlight.

What if he went to get the life jacket right now? No one would ever know. He could sneak out of the tent, follow the trail back to the beginning of the portage and get it. The portage to the campsite had

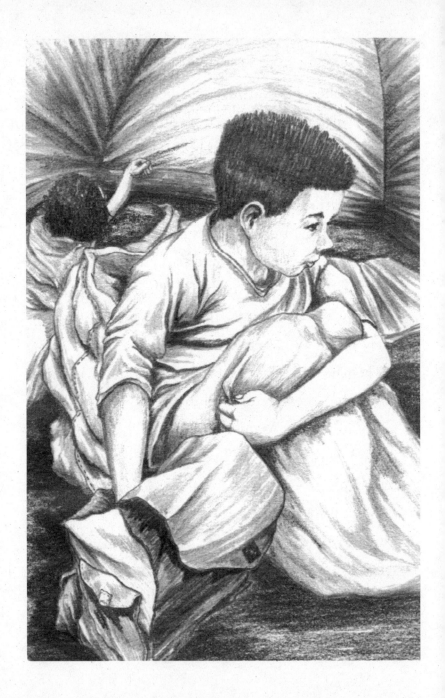

only taken ten or fifteen minutes that afternoon. He could make it to the other lake and back in half an hour. He was sure he could!

But it was dark out there now. And spooky. Anything could be roaming around the woods at this hour of the night. He knew that he shouldn't go out there by himself. The first rule they'd been taught was never to leave the camp alone.

Then he imagined Tim laughing at him. "How could you be so dumb?" Tim would say.

He was tired of being laughed at. He was fed up with being teased. He was not going to let Tim ruin his last day here.

He would do it!

He told his mind to be quiet. He didn't want to hear another word about what a big mistake he was making. He pulled his shorts and a T-shirt out of his pack. He wriggled into them inside his sleeping bag. He grabbed his shoes. He held his breath as he crawled out of the tent. Once he had his runners on, he paused for a moment and looked around. No, he was not going to chicken out now!

He aimed the flashlight at the ground and switched it on. Silent as a ghost, he tiptoed past the other tents to the start of the trail. It was wide and clearly marked. He remembered how easy it had been to follow. He stood still and listened for a moment. There was no sound but silence and the soft lap of a few waves on the beach. The moon was high. The canoes made long shadows where they were lined up along the shore.

Matt shivered. It was scary out here at night. He almost went back to the tent. But he didn't. He gritted his teeth and set out.

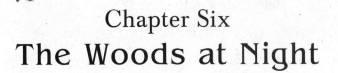

Chapter Six
The Woods at Night

At the edge of the woods it wasn't so bad. Among the trees, though, the darkness grew blacker with every step Matt took. The beam from his flashlight was thin and weak. He tripped over a tree root and dropped the torch. The light went off. It was pitch-dark. He couldn't see a thing!

Matt panicked. He fell to his knees and felt around in the pine needles for the light. It wasn't there. It must have rolled into the bushes. He dug around on the ground beside the path.

Keep calm, he told himself. Keep calm. He had a sick, scared feeling in the pit of his stomach. His hand came across something hard. It was the flashlight. He let out a huge breath of relief.

Then, before he could switch the light back on, something swooped down through the trees and brushed past him. Wings feathered his cheeks. Whatever it was, it was huge! He cried out and crouched down in the dark, his arms over his head.

Whoo! Whoo!

An owl! It was an owl. But what a big one! Matt had no idea owls could be so big. His hands shook as he flicked on the flashlight. He crouched there, too frightened to move.

Should he run back to camp?

No, he couldn't do that. He was almost at the other lake. He must be. He took a deep breath and then another. He stumbled to his feet and brushed leaves and dirt off his knees. He looked around for the owl, but there was no sign of it.

He started forward again. He checked every step for roots or rocks. Then he stepped on a loose stone.

His foot twisted beneath him. He let out a gasp of pain and stopped to catch his breath. He took another step. His foot hurt, but not too badly. It wasn't sprained. He moved on.

He couldn't believe how long it was taking. It was much farther than he had thought. It had been easy walking in the daylight. Dave had been joking. Everybody had been singing. It had taken no time at all to get through the portage. The only things on Matt's mind then were how hot and sweaty he was and how many mosquitoes there were. There were lots more mosquitoes now! He swatted at them with every step he took. The night was alive with them.

Finally the trail began to widen out. Matt sniffed. Could he smell water? He stopped to listen. He was sure he could hear the murmur of small waves hitting the shore. Was he there? Had he made it?

He had!

The trees ended. He was on the edge of the lake. It gleamed silver in the moonlight. He shone his

light around. Something orange hung from a tree, right where he had left it. His life jacket! He raced over and pulled it down from the branch.

I did it! he thought. I'll be back at camp long before dawn. Nobody will know I was ever gone.

Right then his flashlight went out.

Chapter Seven
More Trouble

He couldn't believe it. He pushed the switch up and down. He shook the light. He opened the case, took the batteries out and put them back in. Nothing. The batteries were dead. Just like that.

Then he remembered. He had read in his sleeping bag until late the night before. He had thought he was so smart, curling up with the bag over him so that no light would shine through and give him away.

Not so smart now, he thought. But what could he do? To make matters worse, the moon slipped behind a cloud. Even the open beach was plunged into darkness. Matt stared up at the sky, searching for stars. Clouds had piled up so thickly that there was not a star to be seen. Matt's heart sank. How could he have forgotten that Dave had said rain was on its way?

A cool breeze sprang up. Matt shivered. I am not afraid, he told himself. But he was. He peered into the trees. He could barely see the break in the bush where the trail began. He shoved his flashlight into his pocket and hooked his life jacket over his arm. Then he made his way to the trail opening. He grabbed the nearest tree and leaned forward into the blackness. Could he make out the trail? Yes. He thought he could. All he had to do was follow the path. It would be harder without a light, but as long as he didn't blunder off into the trees he should be all right. He fought down his fear. He had made it here. He could make it back again. Of course he could!

He took one last look back. The clouds still covered the moon and the stars. He felt the first raindrop on his cheek.

I could just curl up under a tree for the night, he thought. As soon as it gets light I could hike back to camp.

But even as he thought it, he knew he couldn't do that. He had to be in his tent when Dave did the morning check.

No, he had to get back. At least in the trees, he wouldn't get as wet.

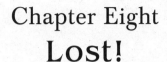

Chapter Eight
Lost!

But it did rain hard.

Within minutes, Matt was soaked. He tried holding the life jacket over his head, but it kept catching on branches. He thought about putting it on, but it was too bulky for walking. Besides, it was soaked now too.

He trudged on, one foot after the other. A couple of times he found himself in the bush. Each time he found the path again.

At least the rain had made the mosquitoes leave him alone. He scratched at a bite on his neck and walked into a tree.

A tree? In the middle of the path?

He tried to go around it to the left. A tangle of bushes got in his way. He tried to go around it on the other side—more bushes. What had happened to the path?

He turned around, took a few steps back and fell over a log. He got to his feet. He must have strayed off the path somehow—there hadn't been a log on the trail before.

Don't panic, he told himself. Just go back a bit. You'll find the path again. But his insides felt hollow. He took a deep breath and inched forward. The way was open for a few steps. Then he found himself pushing aside branches again.

This couldn't be right!

He turned around and backtracked. He'd go back to the log and start out again. But the log wasn't there.

His mouth was dry. His heart was pounding so hard that he thought it would burst out of his chest. He could see nothing but darkness all around him.

He crashed into bushes and trees everywhere he turned. He was lost!

He couldn't help himself. He sank down to his knees with a sob.

In that moment, from somewhere close, he heard the wolf howl.

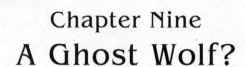

Chapter Nine
A Ghost Wolf?

For the first time in his life, Matt knew terror. He had heard of being frozen with fear. Well, now he was. He could not move. He tried hard to see into the darkness. He tried to hear if the wolf was coming nearer. But he could see nothing, and all he could hear was the sound of raindrops landing all around him. Then, right in front of him, a white form took shape.

The wolf!

What should he do? He couldn't see to run. He couldn't even see if there was a tree close enough to climb. At that moment, the rain stopped. A stray

moonbeam slipped between the trees and struck the wolf. Matt stared at the wolf. The wolf stared back at Matt. Its eyes shone yellow in the moonlight. Matt braced for the attack. He held his life jacket up in front of him.

Not that it will do any good, he thought. He choked back another sob.

The wolf did not spring. It stood there for a long moment. It looked at Matt with its yellow eyes.

It looked as if it wanted to talk to him.

Then it turned away. Matt couldn't believe it. He stared after the animal. The wolf took a few steps, stopped and looked back over its shoulder. Matt still couldn't move. The wolf whined. It took another step and looked back again.

He's trying to tell me something, Matt thought. He wants me to follow him!

Follow a wolf? Into the woods? He would have to be crazy!

But what else could he do? He was lost! Slowly,

Matt got to his feet. He took one small step in after the wolf.

I can't believe I'm doing this, he thought and took another step.

The wolf glowed white in the moonlight as it glided on ahead of him.

Like a ghost.

Matt pushed the thought out of his mind. He was scared enough as it was.

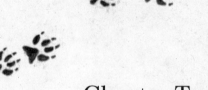

Chapter Ten
The Pup

Matt followed the white wolf through the trees. The wolf paused every now and then. Each time it looked back to make certain that Matt was following. Matt kept his eyes glued on the animal. What if it disappeared as suddenly as it had appeared? Then the wolf turned a bend in the path and was gone.

Matt's stomach clenched. He ran forward. He was in a clearing lit by the full moon. No sign of rain now—the stars shone down hard and bright. The wolf stood at the other side of the clearing. It was waiting for him. Matt paused and looked more closely.

Lying at the wolf's feet, he saw the body of another wolf.

Without thinking, he ran forward. When he reached the animal, Matt knelt. It wasn't a wolf that lay there. It was a dog, a brown-and-white husky kind of a dog. Its leg was caught in the jaws of an iron trap. Matt reached out and touched the dog's fur. It was a female, but she was dead. Matt looked around and caught his breath. A small body lay on the leaves beside its mother. He touched it with one finger. The little animal was cold and stiff.

Matt looked up at the wolf. Was this dog his mate?

"There's nothing I can do," Matt whispered. "They're both dead."

Then he heard a whimper. Something cold and wet thrust itself into the palm of his hand. He looked down. A small pup was nosing up against him. This one was alive!

Matt looked back at the wolf.

"Yours?" he asked. "Is this your pup?"

The wolf's eyes gleamed yellow. He was panting a little—it almost seemed as if his mouth was curved in a smile. Then he turned and, with one last look back at Matt, began to trot away.

Matt tucked his T-shirt into his shorts and nestled the pup down inside the shirt, close to his skin. He cradled the little body with one hand, picked up his life jacket and set out to follow the wolf again. This time he was not afraid.

Chapter Eleven
Safe at Last

The rain held off. Moonlight shone down through the branches of the trees. It seemed to Matt that his feet followed the path all by themselves. He never tripped. He didn't even stumble. The white wolf gleamed in the moonlight as it sped along in front of him. It stopped every now and then and looked back. The pup made small noises but snuggled close to Matt's chest.

Then Matt saw a light. He heard voices. He broke through the last few trees. There in front of him was the camp. The fire had been lit again. Dave and the other counselors were gathered around it. Dave must have checked the tent and found him gone.

The wolf stood quietly in the trees beside Matt and watched. It turned its yellow eyes back to Matt. Then it lowered its head, almost as if it were saying good-bye, and melted back into the woods.

Matt stared after it. A white wolf with yellow eyes. It was just like the one his father had saved. Could it be the same wolf? Could it have known that the son of the man who had once saved its life would now save its pup?

Dave looked up and saw Matt. "There he is!" he cried. He loped across the clearing to where Matt stood.

"What in the world have you been doing?" he shouted. "Where have you been? Man, you are in a pile of trouble!" Then he took a good look at Matt. "What have you got there?" he asked.

Matt untucked his shirt and drew out the pup.

"He needs some milk," he said.

The pup traveled back to camp the next morning, tucked inside Matt's shirt. Matt could feel its small

warm body against his stomach as he paddled the canoe. It gave him strength.

When Matt's dad drove into camp that afternoon, Matt was waiting for him. The pup was nestled in his arms, chewing happily on his shirtsleeve.

"I've got something to show you," he said as his father got out of the car. Matt held out the wiggling, furry, white pup.

"I want you to meet Wolfie," Matt said. "I think you knew his father."

The author of many beloved books for children, **Karleen Bradford** has spent a lot of time camping in the wilderness. She lives in Owen Sound, Ontario.

Orca Echoes

The Paper Wagon
martha attema
Graham Ross, illustrator

The Big Tree Gang
Jo Ellen Bogart
Dean Griffiths, illustrator

Jeremy and the Enchanted Theater
Becky Citra
Jessica Milne, illustrator

Sam and Nate
PJ Sarah Collins
Katherine Jin, illustrator

Down the Chimney with Googol and Googolplex
Nelly Kazenbroot

Under the Sea with Googol and Googolplex
Nelly Kazenbroot

The Birthday Girl
Jean Little
June Lawrason, illustrator

The True Story of George
Ingrid Lee
Stéphane Denis, illustrator

George Most Wanted
Ingrid Lee
Stéphane Denis, illustrator

A Bee in Your Ear
Frieda Wishinsky
Louise-Andrée Laliberté, illustrator

A Noodle Up Your Nose
Frieda Wishinsky
Louise-Andrée Laliberté, illustrator

Dimples Delight
Frieda Wishinsky
Louise-Andrée Laliberté, illustrator